Autumn
Publishing

Published in 2019
by Autumn Publishing
Cottage Farm
Sywell
NN6 0BJ
www.igloobooks.com

LEO002 0319
2 4 6 8 10 9 7 5 3 1
ISBN 978-1-78905-585-6

Printed and manufactured in China

Autumn
Publishing

Minnie is hard at work in her busy Bow-tique. "Oh, Cuckoo-Loca," says Minnie, "isn't my new magic bejeweller fantastic?"

WoW is it
LoveL

W tWins

Suddenly, Minnie hears giggling!
"Who's making that noise?" she says.
"It's us, Aunt Minnie!" shout Millie and
Melody, jumping out at her.

Delighted, Minnie greets her twin nieces.
"Hello, Millie! Hello, Melody!"
The girls begin to run around the Bow-tique.

Oh, no! They accidentally knock over boxes of bows and beads!

"Can we help you make stuff today?" Millie asks.

"We promise to be extra good," adds Melody.

Cuckoo-Loca looks at the mess the girls have already made. "Famous last words," she says.

"I was just thinking how nice it would be to have two helpers today," says Minnie. "Why don't you unpack that box of ribbons for me?"

"Yay!" shout Millie and Melody.

Just then, Daisy Duck rushes into the shop.

"Minnie!" she calls excitedly. "You're never going to believe it…"

Oops-a-daisy! She slips on the spilled beads and falls!

"Oh, Daisy!" cries Minnie. "Are you alright?"

"Never better," says Daisy. "Guess what famous movie superstar is on her way over to the Bow-tique right now?"

"Penelope Poodle?" guesses Minnie.

"Right!" cries Daisy. "I've just got off the phone with her people. They made me promise that Penelope could shop in total peace and quiet."

Suddenly, Millie and Melody
zoom past Daisy, nearly
knocking her over.

"Hi, Daisy," the twins shout.
"Sorry about the beads!"

Daisy looks at the girls and
sighs. "Minnie, the twins are
not total peace and quiet."

Minnie giggles. "Normally, that's true.
But they've promised to be extra good today."
  Millie and Melody reach for some spools of
colourful ribbon.

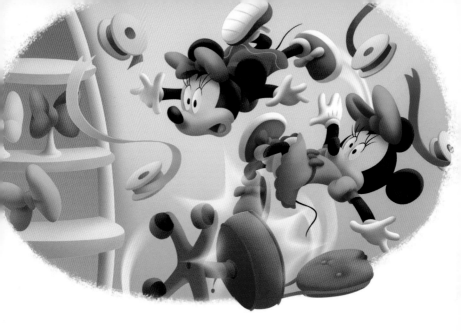

Uh-oh! Looks like the helpers
need some help!

"Oops! Sorry, Aunt Minnie!"

Just then, they hear a huge commotion outside.

Penelope Poodle has arrived!

Photographers and excited fans crowd around the famous movie star. "Look this way, Miss Poodle," shouts a photographer. "Can we get a smile?"

"Oh!" cries Daisy. "She's here!"

Daisy hurries to clean up the mess.

The glamorous Penelope Poodle glides
through the door.

"Welcome to my Bow-tique," says Minnie.

"Hello," says Penelope. "You must help me.
I'm accepting a Golden Bone award in less than an
hour, and I need something fabulous to wear!"

Suddenly, Millie and Melody race past Penelope!
"Beep, beep!" shouts Millie.
"Coming through!" warns Melody.

Penelope Poodle gasps. "I was promised that I could shop in total peace and quiet."

Cuckoo-Loca pops up to snap a picture. "Love your movies. Even the bad ones. May I have your autograph?"

"Not now, Cuckoo-Loca," Daisy says firmly. "Minnie was just about to show Miss Poodle that one-of-a-kind thing she made."

Penelope Poodle perks up. "One-of-a-kind?"

Thinking fast, Minnie picks up the sparkly bow she made with her magic bejeweller and shows it to Penelope.

"I call it the Glitterati," says Minnie.

Penelope Poodle is very impressed.

Suddenly, Millie and Melody crash into
some of Minnie's bow displays!
"Look out!" shout the twins.

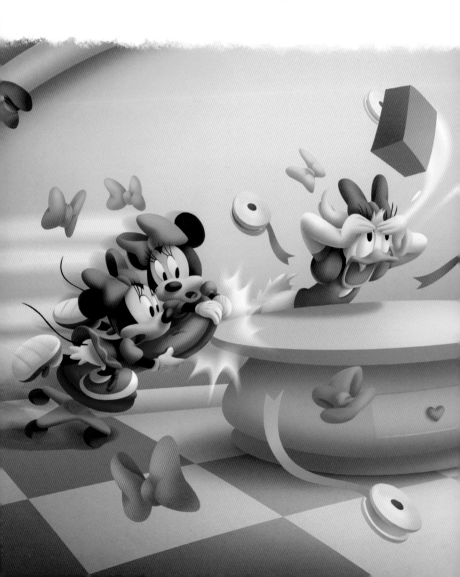

They knock over racks of bows, ribbons and even a can of paint.
The paint splatters everywhere!

Penelope Poodle has had enough. "I can see that coming here was a mistake."

"I am positive I can find you something gorgeous to wear," Minnie says, "if you'll just wait."

"Wait?" says Penelope. "I can't waste another
moment! I simply must go!" Suddenly, Millie and
Melody wrap Penelope in pink ribbons. "What
have those little monsters done to me?"

"Oh, they're not little monsters," says Minnie. "They're little helpers!"

She quickly adds bows and jewels to the twins' handiwork. "I think they're on to something!"

Penelope Poodle looks in the mirror.
"I look fabulous!" she says. "You're brilliant!"
Minnie smiles sweetly.
"That's what I always say," Daisy agrees.

Everyone loves Penelope's new outfit.

"Miss Poodle!" calls a fan. "That's a fantastic look!"

"Who are you wearing?" asks a photographer.

Penelope smiles. "Who else? Minnie Mouse, of course!"

Millie and Melody look at the mess they have made in the Bow-tique.

"We'll clean up for you, Aunt Minnie," they promise.

Daisy lets out a sigh of relief. "I don't know how you do it," she says, shaking her head.

"Oh, Daisy," says Minnie, "I'm just trying to spread happiness, one bow at a time."